MY FIRST

Raggedy Ann

Raggedy Ann's Wishing Pebble

MY FIRST

Raggedy

Ann

Raggedy Ann's Wishing Pebble

ADAPTED FROM THE STORY BY

JOHNNY GRUELLE

ILLUSTRATED BY JAN PALMER

ALADDIN PAPERBACKS

NEW YORK LONDON TORONTO SYDNEY SINGAPORE

Aladdin Paperbacks
An imprint of Simon & Schuster
Children's Publishing Division
1230 Avenue of the Americas
New York, NY 10020

Also available in a Simon & Schuster Books for Young Readers hardcover edition.

Book design by Lee Wade
The text of this book was set in Adobe Jenson.
The illustrations were rendered in Winsor and Newton ink and watercolor.

The Library of Congress has cataloged the hardcover edition as follows:
My first Raggedy Ann : Raggedy Ann's wishing pebble / adapted from the story by Johnny Gruelle ;
illustrated by Jan Palmer. –1st ed.
p. cm.
Summary: With the help of their animal friends, Raggedy Ann and Andy
try to retrieve the magic wishing pebble stolen by the mischievous Minky.
ISBN 0-689-82173-5 (hc.)
[1. Dolls—Fiction. 2. Magic—Fiction. 3. Wishes—Fiction. 4. Animals—Fiction.]
I. Gruelle, Johnny, 1880?-1938. Raggedy Ann stories. II. Palmer, Jan, ill.
[Fic]—dc21
98-16793
ISBN 0-689-85117-0 (Aladdin pbk.)

Printed in the United States of America

The History of Raggedy Ann

One day, a little girl named Marcella discovered an old rag doll in her attic. Because Marcella was often ill and had to spend much of her time at home, her father, a writer named Johnny Gruelle, looked for ways to keep her entertained. He was inspired by Marcella's rag doll, which had bright shoe-button eyes and red-yarn hair. The doll became known as Raggedy Ann.

Knowing how much Marcella adored Raggedy Ann, Johnny Gruelle wrote stories about the doll. He later collected the stories he had written for Marcella and published them in a series of books. He gave Raggedy Ann a brother, Raggedy Andy, and over the years the two rag dolls acquired many friends.

Raggedy Ann has been an important part of Americana for more than half a century, as well as a treasured friend to many generations of readers. After all, she is much more than a rag doll—she is a symbol of caring and love, of compassion and generosity. Her magical world is one that promises to delight children of all ages for years to come.

Raggedy Ann and Andy were rag dolls stuffed with nice white cotton. They had bright shoe-button eyes and happy smiles painted on their rag faces. One day they were poking about by the Looking Glass Brook when Raggedy Andy held up a round white pebble. "Do you think this is a wishing pebble?" he asked.

"I have no idea," said Raggedy Ann. "Let's make a wish."

"Why don't we wish for something for our friends, the Muskrats?" Raggedy Andy asked. "They always give us Muskrat bread and butter when we visit."

Raggedy Ann and Andy both squeezed the pebble as hard as they could and Raggedy Ann said, "I wish the Muskrats had a magic soda-water fountain right in their living room." They agreed that it was a good wish, and then they went to sleep in the sun.

The dolls were awakened a little later by Freddy Fieldmouse.

"There's a magic soda-water fountain in the Muskrats' home," he exclaimed. "They're inviting everyone for ice-cream sodas!" He scampered off.

"That means the wishing pebble was real!" Raggedy Ann said. "Let's go see the fountain." She buried the pebble in the sand before heading off to the Muskrats.

Raggedy Ann and Andy found a crowd of animals at the Muskrats' home, all drinking sodas. When the dolls told them about the magic wishing pebble, Mister and Missus Muskrat thanked them for their kindness. Missus Muskrat snipped a hole in the center of each doll's mouth, so they could try the sodas for themselves.

"Whee!" Raggedy Ann cried, after she and Andy drank fifteen ice-cream sodas. "I don't believe I can drink another one. Let's go find the wishing pebble that I buried in the sand."

"That's a fine idea," cried Missus Muskrat. She and the other animals and the dolls ran to the brook. They hunted in the loose sand on the bank, but they couldn't find the wishing pebble.

Mister Muskrat had stayed home to wash the soda glasses, but now he ran to join them. "It's gone!" he cried. "The magic fountain just disappeared!"

"Of course it's gone," a voice sounded from across the brook.

"Who is that?" Raggedy Andy shouted.

"Ha! Ha!" said the voice, "I saw where Raggedy Ann buried the wishing pebble. I took it and wished the magic soda fountain would disappear from the Muskrats' house. Now I have the fountain and the wishing pebble too!"

Missus Muskrat couldn't keep from crying. "I had planned on all of our friends helping themselves to ice-cream sodas from the magic fountain," she sobbed.

Mister Muskrat wiped his eyes. "It's so nice to have a cold ice-cream soda on a hot day."

"Don't cry," said Raggedy Ann. "We'll get the pebble back."

While the animals were comforting the Muskrats, Raggedy Ann and Andy slipped away and crossed the brook. They got a little wet, but they soon dried in the sunshine.

"Do you know what?" asked Raggedy Ann. "I'll bet whoever has the wishing pebble can't make the fountain work because he is so unkind."

"Stop talking about me!" said the mysterious voice. "I'll bet you two old rag dolls are the reason my sodas taste like burnt candy!"

Raggedy Ann and Andy ignored the voice and walked along the bank, looking for clues to the missing pebble. Just as they passed under a large tree, a big checkered tablecloth fell down on top of their heads. Before they could untangle themselves, their feet were tied together by a little man with thin legs and a long nose. And when he spoke, they recognized the mysterious voice. It was Minky, who was known by everyone for his tricks and pranks.

"Ha!" said Minky. "I'm not letting you go until you tell me how to use the wishing pebble. I need a new magic fountain with soda that tastes sweet!"

"Selfish man!" Raggedy Ann laughed at Minky. "The wishing pebble only brings good things when you wish for something nice for others."

Suddenly Minky let out a howl and fell onto the grass. "Something is biting me!" Tears streamed down his face as he got to his feet and ran away.

"There!" Clifton Crawdad appeared suddenly, rubbing his big claws together. "Minky filled my doorway with mud one day, and it took me a long time to clean it out. Now I've pinched him with my claws, so we're even."

He quickly untied the dolls.

"Thank you!" said Raggedy Andy. "We'd better find Minky."

"It's no trouble," Clifton said, and burrowed back into his mud house.

Raggedy Ann and Andy crossed the brook again and ran into Winnie Woodchuck.

"What happened?" she asked. "You're soaking wet! Come inside this minute." She hustled Raggedy Ann and Andy inside their home, and Walter Woodchuck made them comfortable in front of the crackly fire. They sat and drank licorice tea and ate Woodchuck cookies, which are made from twigs and hazelnuts.

Suddenly the door burst open and Minky stomped inside. "Give me those cookies!" he shouted.

"Now you march right out, Mister Minky!" said Winnie Woodchuck. "You are very rude."

But before he could leave, Raggedy Andy said, "That pebble belongs to us!" He grabbed Minky by his jacket.

"Stop, Andy!" cried Raggedy Ann. "Now *you're* being mean. And when you're unkind, the wishing pebble won't work properly. That's why Minky's sodas aren't sweet." Raggedy Andy let go of Minky, and the little man ran out the door.

It was quiet for a minute, then Raggedy Ann's shoe-button eyes twinkled and she whispered, "I'll bet Minky is listening outside the window."

Walter Woodchuck smiled. "Let's go outside and look for the magic lollipop garden," he said loudly. "Someone told me it's growing in the grass by the brook."

The Woodchucks and the dolls snuck down to the brook, where Minky was crawling in the long grass. "What are you looking for?" asked Raggedy Ann.

"You know perfectly well!" Minky replied angrily. "Go away. The magic lollipops are mine!" Then he slipped in the muddy grass and fell into the deepest part of the brook.

Minky couldn't swim very well, so Raggedy Ann held out a long stick to him and pulled him ashore. "Why are you so kind when I was mean to you?" the little man asked. Water dripped from his jacket and long nose. "It was wrong of me to take your lovely wishing pebble. It's just that none of the animals like me, so I wanted to play a trick on them." He sniffed loudly.

Raggedy Ann smiled. "Don't feel sad, Minky," she said. She held out the wishing pebble, which had fallen from Minky's pocket. "I just wished the soda fountain was back at the Muskrats. And I wished for a lollipop garden in your backyard. I'll bet if you bring the Muskrats some lollipops, they'll give you a soda and let you stay for dinner. They're really very nice once you get to know them."

While Minky went to look for his new lollipop garden, Raggedy Ann and Andy decided to try one last soda at the Muskrat's house. On their way home they passed Minky digging in his garden. They waved good-bye, and then left to join their friends in the nursery.